Heroes, Horses, and Harvest Moons

Illustrated Reader

A Cornucopia of Best-Loved Poems

Edited and Introduced by
Jim Weiss

Illustrations & Book Design by
Crystal Cregge

Copyright 2018 Well-Trained Mind Press

All rights reserved

Printed in the United States of America

No part of this work may be reproduced or transmitted in any form or by any means, electronic or mechanical, including photocopying and recording, or by any information storage or retrieval system without prior written permission of the copyright owner unless such copying is expressly permitted by federal copyright law.

Address requests for permissions to support@welltrainedmind.com or Well-Trained Mind Press, Attention: Permissions, 18021 the Glebe Lane, Charles City, VA 23030.

Publisher's Cataloging-In-Publication Data
(Prepared by The Donohue Group, Inc.)

Names: Weiss, Jim, editor, writer of supplementary textual content. | Cregge, Crystal, illustrator, designer.
Title: Heroes, horses, and harvest moons illustrated reader / illustrations and book design by Crystal Cregge ; edited and introduced by Jim Weiss.
Description: [Charles City, Virginia] : Well-Trained Mind Press, [2018] | Series: A cornucopia of best-loved poems ; [1] | Interest age level: 5 and up. | A word-for-word transcript of the audiobook produced in 2017. | Summary: "In this new book, master storyteller Jim Weiss introduces children to 40 classic poems, and provides informative profiles of the poets, including Emily Dickinson, Walt Whitman, e.e. cummings, and many more."–Provided by publisher.
Identifiers: ISBN 9781945841217 | ISBN 9781945841224 (ebook)
Subjects: LCSH: Poetry. | Nursery rhymes. | CYAC: Poetry. | Nursery rhymes.
Classification: LCC PN6101 .H47 2018 (print) | LCC PN6101 (ebook) | DDC 808.81–dc23

For more literature, history, math, grammar, and writing books and audio resources, visit
welltrainedmind.com

CONTENT

Preface 1

Nursery Rhymes and Poems 2
from Mother Goose:

   Little Jack Horner
   Wee Willie Winkie
   There Was a Crooked Man
   Three Men in a Tub
   Old King Cole
   Hey Diddle Diddle
   Little Miss Muffet
   Peter Piper
   One Misty, Moisty Morning

Poems About Nature: 8
About Robert Frost

   The Pasture *(Frost)*

About Robert Louis Stevenson 10

   Windy Nights *(Stevenson)*

Who Has Seen the Wind? *(Rossetti)* 11

About Christina Rossetti 11

   Clouds *(Rossetti)*

About Edna St. Vincent Millay 12

   Afternoon on a Hill *(Millay)*

About William Butler Yeats 13

   The Lake Isle of Innisfree *(Yeats)*

About Carl Sandburg 14

   Theme in Yellow *(Sandburg)*
   Fog *(Sandburg)*

About Emily Dickinson 15

   To Make a Prairie *(Dickinson)*
   I Send Two Sunsets *(Dickinson)*

About E.E. Cummings 16

   In Just *(Cummings)*
   Little Tree *(Cummings)* 17

Wild Ride #1: 18
About Henry Wadsworth Longfellow

   Paul Revere's Ride *(Longfellow)*

All-American Poems: 22
About Walt Whitman

   I Hear America Singing *(Whitman)*

About Ernest Thayer 24

   Casey at the Bat *(Thayer)*

Unusual Companions: 26

   The Bean-Stalk

About John Kendrick Bangs 28

   The Little Elf *(Bangs)*

The Song of the Wandering Aengus ... 29
(Yeats)

Poems that Take Flight: 30

   The Eagle *(Tennyson)*

About Rachel Field 32

   Something Told the Wild Geese *(Field)*

The Swing *(Stevenson)* 33

Inspiration: 34
About Edgar A. Guest

   It Couldn't be Done *(Guest)*

Wild Ride #2: 36
About Alfred, Lord Tennyson

   The Charge of the Light Brigade *(Tennyson)*

Sensible Nonsense: 38
About A.A. Milne

   Jonathan Jo *(Milne)*

The King's Breakfast *(Milne)* 40

About Vachel Lindsay 42

   The Moon's the North Wind's Cooky *(Lindsay)*

About Edward Lear 43

   The Pobble Who Has No Toes *(Lear)*

Bedtime and Dreamtime: 44

   Bed in Summer *(Stevenson)*

About Thomas Hood 46

   In The Summer When I Go to Bed *(Hood)*

About Eugene Field 48

   Wynken, Blynken, and Nod *(Field)*

About Leigh Hunt 50

   Abou Ben Adhem *(Hunt)*

Conclusion 53

FOREWORD

By Susan Wise Bauer

This illustrated Companion Reader is an exact transcript of the poetry anthology *Heroes, Horses, and Harvest Moons,* as selected, introduced, and performed by storyteller Jim Weiss.

The wonderful poems in the anthology are selected for their beauty, vivid vocabulary, complex sentence structure, rich images, and imaginative power. This Companion Reader can certainly be used on its own as an introduction to the world's great poetry, but combined with the audio version, it gives you the opportunity to enhance your child's language skills.

Language, both written and oral, is most easily and thoroughly learned when *heard, read,* and *spoken.*

Hear Jim performing the poems by listening to the anthology on CD or MP3. (See welltrainedmind.com for a full listing and instantly downloadable digital versions!)

Read along with the performance. Students can improve their reading fluency, vocabulary, and their understanding of punctuation, sentence structure, and grammar by following along as Jim performs these words. Even students who are not reading at the level represented in this book can be moved forward in reading competency by reading along as Jim speaks the words. The beautiful illustrations add an additional dimension to the student's appreciation of poetic language, by providing a nonverbal interpretation that clarifies and supports the written world of the poems.

Say the words. The final element in language learning is to *speak* great words and sentences out loud. Ask the child to memorize selected poems, and then perform them!

Continued

Foreword continued

Memorization and recitation of poetry exercises the child's memory, stores sophisticated and expressive language in her mind, and provides early training in public speaking.

Here's a suggested method: First, ask the child to listen to the chosen poem five times in a row, until she or he can chime in with many of the lines.

Second, ask the child to read the poem out loud five times per day.

Third, ask the child to recite the poem all alone, to a mirror or to stuffed animals, with the Companion Reader open in front of him or her, only glancing down if memory fails.

Finally, ask the child to perform the poem in front of you—or, for the very brave, in front of selected family and friends!

TRACK 1

Well Trained Mind Press presents: Jim Weiss's recording of Heroes, Horses, and Harvest Moons: A Cornucopia of Best-Loved Poems, Volume One. Performed and compiled by Jim Weiss.

PREFACE

The word "poetry" comes from a very old Greek word that means "to move." Reading or listening to poetry is supposed to move us, to change us, to introduce new ways of seeing things. Sometimes the subjects are people or things from places and times different from our own. Poems such as these can show us what we have in common with those other people and their ways of living. Other poems are all about things we find around ourselves every day and which we're so used to that we pay hardly any attention to them. A good poet will have us noticing what we ignored before. A great poet will do that while also touching our emotions so that we never again look at that everyday object in the same old way. All the poems in this collection do that.

In choosing which ones to read to you, I decided to read only poems written in the English language, and generally using words that we might use ourselves in conversation. You'll hear also a little bit about each poet. You'll hear from men and women who lived and wrote in England, Scotland, Ireland, India, and the United States. I hope this will lead you to find more poems from these and other authors, and perhaps to trying your own hand at writing poetry. Either way, I hope you have fun.

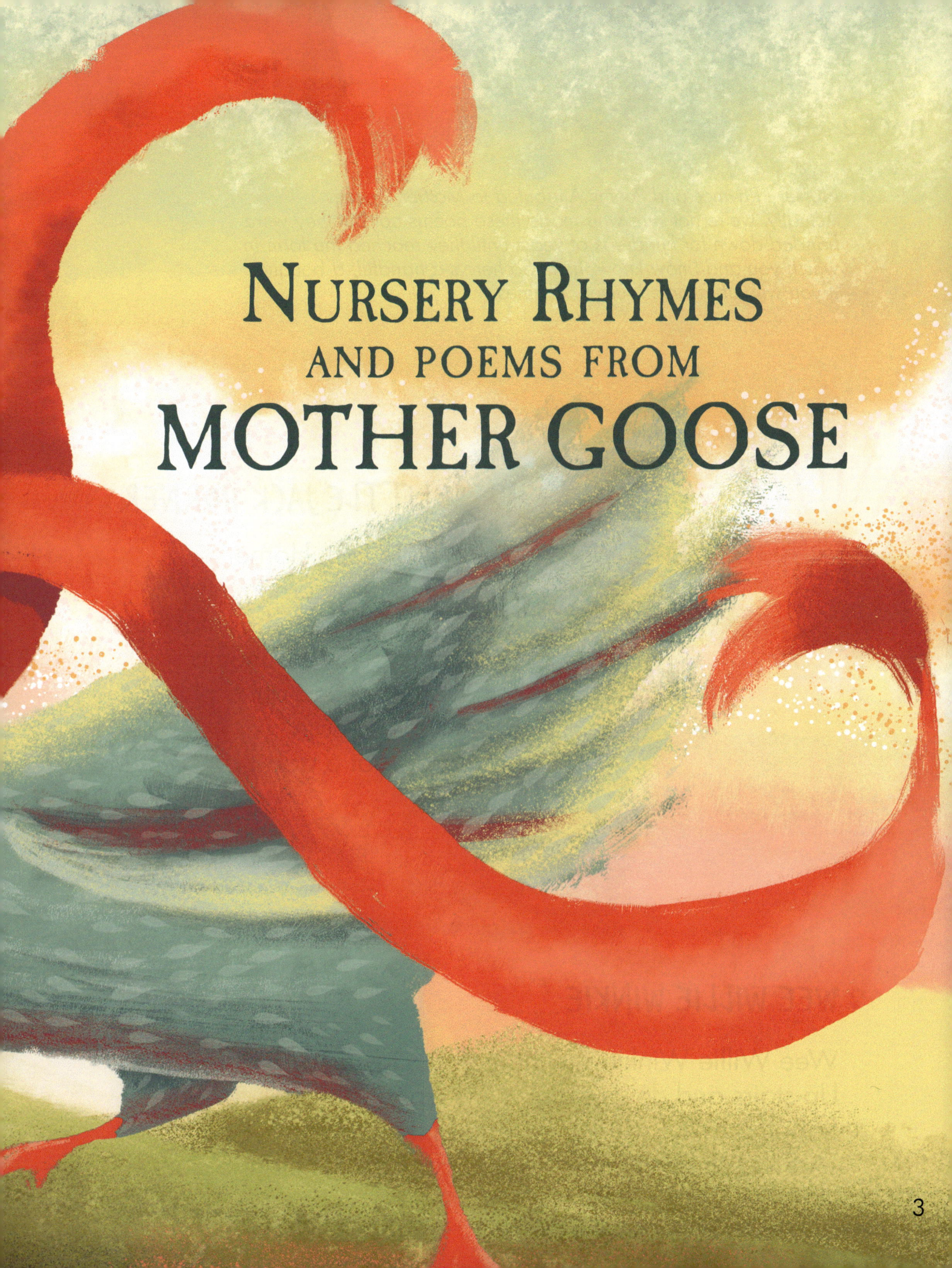

Nursery Rhymes and Poems from Mother Goose

TRACK 2

*Nursery Rhymes and Poems Attributed to Mother Goose.
Actually, we're not sure who made these poems up. But they were handed down for hundreds of years until they reached the form in which you and I now know them. So here's a handful, a bouquet if you will, of favorite Nursery Rhymes.*

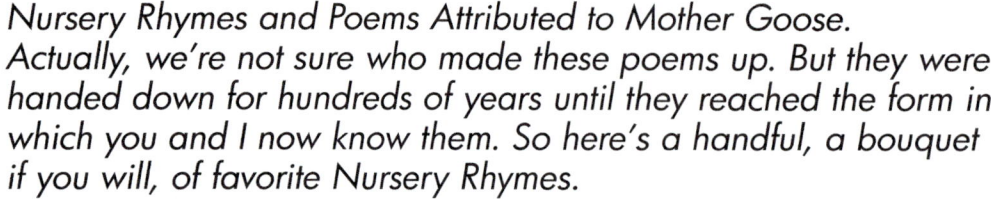

LITTLE JACK HORNER

Little Jack Horner
Sat in a corner,
   Eating a Christmas pie;
He put in his thumb,
And pulled out a plum,
   And said,
"What a good boy am I!"

WEE WILLIE WINKIE

Wee Willie Winkie ran through the town,
Up stairs and down stairs in his night-gown,
Rapping at the window, crying at the lock,
"Are the children in their beds? For now it's eight o'clock!"

THERE WAS A CROOKED MAN

There was a crooked man, and he went a crooked mile.
He found a crooked sixpence against a crooked stile.
He bought a crooked cat, which caught a crooked mouse,
And they all lived together in a crooked little house.

THREE MEN IN A TUB

Rub-a-dub-dub,
Three men in a tub,
And who do you think were there?
The butcher, the baker, the candlestick maker,
And all had come from the fair.

OLD KING COLE

Old King Cole was a merry old soul,
And a merry old soul was he;
He called for his pipe,
and he called for his bowl,
And he called for his fiddlers three.
Every fiddler he had a fiddle,
Twee-diddle twee-diddle twee-dee,
Oh there's none so rare, as can compare,
With King Cole and his fiddlers three.

HEY DIDDLE DIDDLE

Hey diddle diddle,
 The cat and the fiddle,
The cow jumped over the moon.
 The little dog laughed,
To see such sport,
 And the dish ran away with the spoon.

LITTLE MISS MUFFET

Little Miss Muffet
Sat on her tuffet
Eating her curds and whey;
Along came a spider
And sat down beside her
And frightened Miss Muffet away.

PETER PIPER

Peter Piper picked a peck of pickled peppers.
A peck of pickled peppers Peter Piper picked.
If Peter Piper picked a peck of pickled peppers,
Where's the peck of pickled peppers Peter Piper picked?

ONE MISTY, MOISTY MORNING

One misty, moisty morning,
when cloudy was the weather,
I chanced to meet an old man clad all in leather.
He began to compliment and I began to grin,
    How do you do?
    How do you do?
    and how do you do again?

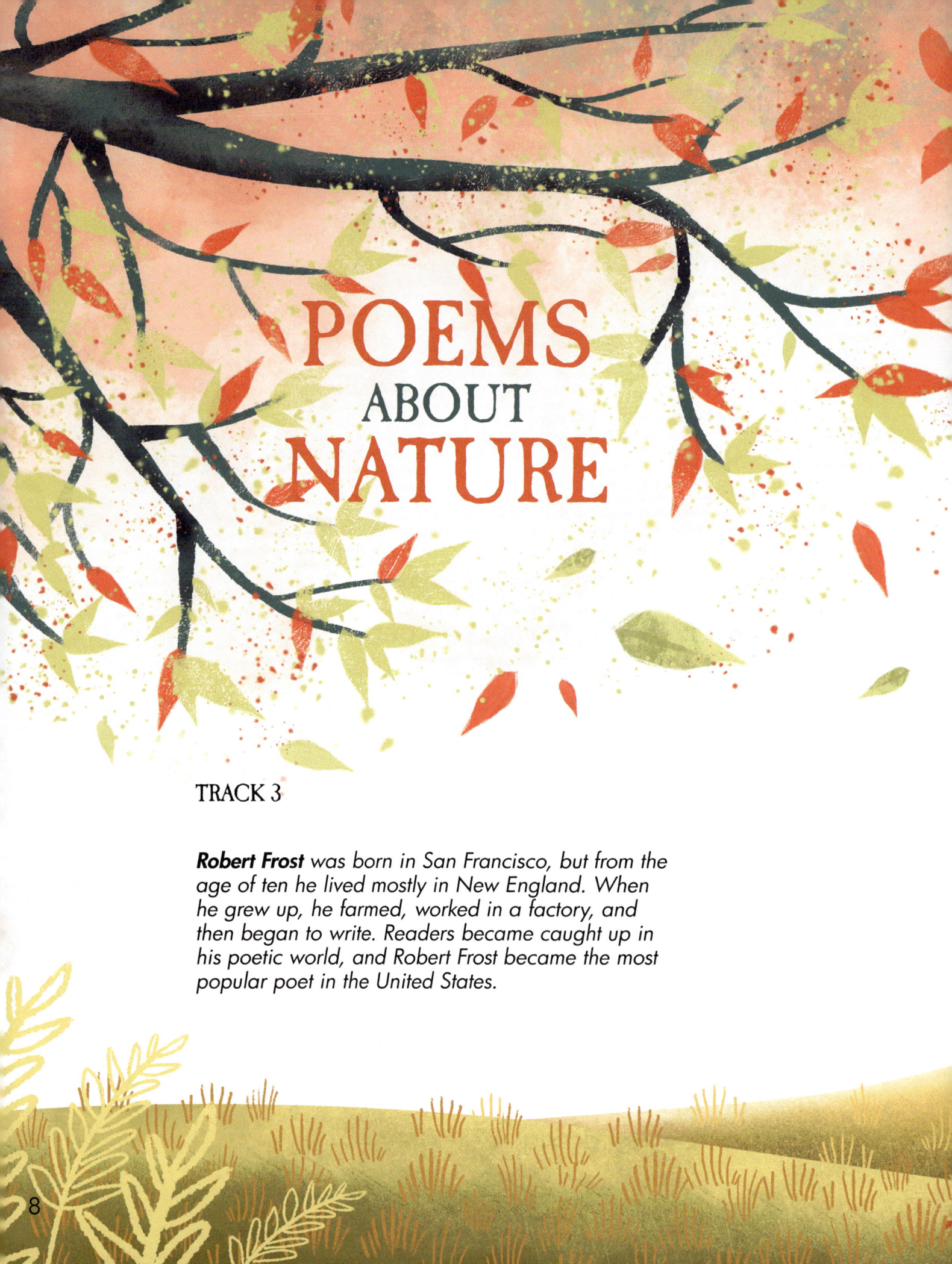

POEMS ABOUT NATURE

TRACK 3

Robert Frost was born in San Francisco, but from the age of ten he lived mostly in New England. When he grew up, he farmed, worked in a factory, and then began to write. Readers became caught up in his poetic world, and Robert Frost became the most popular poet in the United States.

In 1961, when his fellow New Englander John Kennedy became president of the United States, Kennedy invited Robert Frost to read a poem at the inauguration—the ceremony at which Kennedy was sworn in as president. But the bright sunlight made the words on the paper hard to read, so Robert Frost simply set the paper aside and recited another poem from memory.

THE PASTURE
by Robert Frost

I'm going out to clean the pasture spring;
I'll only stop to rake the leaves away
(And wait to watch the water clear, I may):
I sha'n't be gone long. — You come too.

I'm going out to fetch the little calf
That's standing by the mother. It's so young,
It totters when she licks it with her tongue.
I sha'n't be gone long. — You come too.

TRACK 4

Robert Louis Stevenson was born into a wealthy family in Scotland. Almost from birth he faced life-threatening illnesses, and at one point in his childhood, he had to spend an entire year confined to his bed. The nurse his family hired to care for him loved stories and poetry, and she read constantly to the boy.

Well, Stevenson grew up to lead an adventurous life and to write the classic adventure novels Treasure Island and Kidnapped. He also wrote a much-loved book of poetry: A Child's Garden of Verses. And he dedicated it to his childhood nurse. You may wish to compare Stevenson's poem here, "Windy Nights," with the poem that follows it.

WINDY NIGHTS
by Robert Louis Stevenson

Whenever the moon and stars are set,
Whenever the wind is high,
All night long in the dark and wet,
    A man goes riding by.
Late in the night when the fires are out,
Why does he gallop and gallop about?

Whenever the trees are crying aloud,
    And ships are tossed at sea,
By, on the highway, low and loud,
    By at the gallop goes he.
By at the gallop he goes, and then
By he comes back at the gallop again.

TRACK 5

WHO HAS SEEN THE WIND?
by Christina Rossetti

Who has seen the wind?
   Neither I nor you:
But when the leaves hang trembling,
   The wind is passing through.

Who has seen the wind?
   Neither you nor I:
But when the trees bow down their heads,
   The wind is passing by.

TRACK 6

Christina Rossetti, her brother, and their closest friends, all of them writers or painters, all lived in a neighborhood in London with a name that's just perfect for an artist's home: Bloomsbury.

CLOUDS
by Christina Rossetti

White sheep, white sheep,
On a blue hill,
When the wind stops,
You all stand still.
When the wind blows,
You walk away slow.
White sheep, white sheep,
Where do you go?

TRACK 7

Edna St. Vincent Millay was a beautiful woman who could write like an angel, and in the first half of the 1900s her poems, and her public readings of them, lifted her up from a poor childhood and made her famous and wealthy. Ms. Millay once wrote that in life, the thing to do was to "depart" (that is, set out on a journey), "be lost, but climb."

AFTERNOON ON A HILL
by Edna St. Vincent Millay

I will be the gladdest thing
Under the sun!
I will touch a hundred flowers
And not pick one.

I will look at cliffs and clouds
With quiet eyes,
Watch the wind bow down the grass,
And the grass rise.

And when lights begin to show
Up from the town,
I will mark which must be mine,
And then start down!

*Born and raised in Ireland at a time when Ireland was controlled by the English, **William Butler Yeats** set out to remind the Irish of their own traditions. His writing helped them to unite as a people. "The Lake Isle of Innisfree" is about someone in the city thinking about the quiet life of the Irish countryside.*

THE LAKE ISLE OF INNISFREE
by William Butler Yeats

I will arise and go now, and go to Innisfree,
And a small cabin build there, of clay and wattles made:
Nine bean-rows will I have there, a hive for the honey-bee;
And live alone in the bee-loud glade.

And I shall have some peace there, for peace comes dropping slow,
Dropping from the veils of the morning to where the cricket sings;
There midnight's all a glimmer, and noon a purple glow,
And evening full of the linnet's wings.

I will arise and go now, for always night and day
I hear lake water lapping with low sounds by the shore;
While I stand on the roadway, or on the pavements grey,
I hear it in the deep heart's core.

TRACK 9

Carl Sandburg's life was a constant surprise. Born on the wide Midwestern plains, he became a newspaper writer, a guitar-toting traveler who journeyed into backwoods communities and prairie towns to collect old folk songs that might otherwise have been forgotten, the author of a world-famous two-volume book of Abraham Lincoln's life, and most famously, a beloved poet.

Theme in Yellow
by Carl Sandburg

I spot the hills
With yellow balls in autumn.
I light the prairie cornfields
Orange and tawny gold clusters
And I am called pumpkins.
On the last of October
When dusk is fallen
Children join hands
And circle round me
Singing ghost songs
And love to the harvest moon;
I am a jack-o'-lantern
With terrible teeth
And the children know I am fooling.

TRACK 10

Fog
by Carl Sandburg

The fog comes
on little cat feet.

It sits looking
over harbor and city
on silent haunches
and then moves on.

TRACK 11

*The poet **Emily Dickinson** was almost unknown in her own time. From the time she was an adult, she almost never ventured outside her family home and her yard, and yet Emily Dickinson managed to write as if she had experienced people and places the world over.*

It took seventy years after she died for anything like a complete collection of Dickinson's poetry to appear. Today, Emily Dickinson is one of the most widely read and widely loved poets in the world.

To Make A Prairie
by Emily Dickinson

To make a prairie
it takes a clover and one bee,
One clover, and a bee.
And revery.
The revery alone will do,
If bees are few.

TRACK 12

I Send Two Sunsets
by Emily Dickinson

I send Two Sunsets—
Day and I—in competition ran—
I finished Two—and several Stars—
While He—was making One—

His own was ampler—but as I
Was saying to a friend—
Mine—is the more convenient
To Carry in the Hand—

TRACK 13

Edward Estlin Cummings, who signed his poetry e. e. cummings, often broke poems into pieces and put them back somewhat out of order, in an attempt to make readers really look at and think about what the phrases meant. Cummings' poetry surprised and delighted readers as the poetry of no other writer had ever done, and on one famous occasion, as he stepped onstage, the audience surprised him for once by reciting together one of his poems.

In Just
by e. e. cummings

in Just-
spring   when the world is mud-
luscious the little
lame balloonman

whistles   far   and wee

and eddieandbill come
running from marbles and
piracies and it's
spring

when the world is puddle-wonderful

the queer
old balloonman whistles
far   and   wee
and bettyandisbel come dancing

from hop-scotch and jump-rope and

it's
spring
and

      the

         goat-footed

balloonMan   whistles
far
and
wee

TRACK 14

Little Tree
by e. e. cummings

little tree
little silent Christmas tree
you are so little
you are more like a flower

who found you in the green forest
and were you very sorry to come away?
see   i will comfort you
because you smell so sweetly

i will kiss your cool bark
and hug you safe and tight
just as your mother would,
only don't be afraid

look   the spangles
that sleep all the year in a dark box
dreaming of being taken out and allowed to shine,
the balls the chains red and gold the fluffy threads,

put up your little arms
and i'll give them all to you to hold
every finger shall have its ring
and there won't be a single place dark or unhappy

then when you're quite dressed
you'll stand in the window for everyone to see
and how they'll stare!
oh but you'll be very proud

and my little sister and i will take hands
and looking up at our beautiful tree
we'll dance and sing
"Noel Noel"

TRACK 15

And now for the first of two wild rides in our collection: Paul Revere's Ride.

Now here's a wonderful name: **Henry Wadsworth Longfellow.** Longfellow was an enormously popular American poet of the 1800s. In part this was because Longfellow's poems were perfect for reading out loud, and in an age before television, computers, movies, and other electronic media, entertainment meant music or poetry readings in one's home. Well, Longfellow was the fellow for that. "Paul Revere's Ride" tells a true story from the American Revolutionary War.

Paul Revere's Ride
by Henry Wadsworth Longfellow

Listen, my children, and you shall hear
Of the midnight ride of Paul Revere,
On the eighteenth of April, in Seventy-Five:
Hardly a man is now alive
Who remembers that famous day and year.

He said to his friend, "If the British march
By land or sea from the town to-night,
Hang a lantern aloft in the belfry arch
Of the North Church tower, as a signal-light,
One if by land, and two if by sea;
And I on the opposite shore will be,
Ready to ride and spread the alarm
Through every Middlesex village and farm,
For the country folk to be up and to arm."
Then he said "Good night!" and with
　　muffled oar
Silently rowed to the Charlestown shore,
Just as the moon rose over the bay,
Where swinging wide at her moorings lay
The *Somerset*, British man-of-war;
A phantom ship, with each mast and spar
Across the moon, like a prison-bar,
And a huge black hulk, that was magnified
By its own reflection in the tide.

Meanwhile, his friend, through alley and
　　street
Wanders and watches with eager ears,
Till in the silence around him he hears
The muster of men at the barrack door,
The sound of arms, and the tramp of feet,
And the measured tread of the grenadiers
Marching down to their boats on the shore.

Then he climbed to the tower of the church,
Up the wooden stairs, with stealthy tread,
To the belfry-chamber overhead,
And startled the pigeons from their perch
On the sombre rafters, that round him made
Masses and moving shapes of shade,
By the trembling ladder, steep and tall,
To the highest window in the wall,
Where he paused to listen and look down
A moment on the roofs of the town,
And the moonlight flowing over all.
Beneath, in the churchyard, lay the dead,
In their night-encampment on the hill,
Wrapped in silence so deep and still
That he could hear, like a sentinel's tread,

The watchful night-wind, as it went
Creeping along from tent to tent,
And seeming to whisper, "All is well!"
A moment only he feels the spell
Of the place and the hour, and the secret
      dread
Of the lonely belfry and the dead;
For suddenly all his thoughts are bent
On a shadowy something far away,
Where the river widens to meet the bay,
A line of black, it bends and floats
On the rising tide, like a bridge of boats.

Meanwhile, impatient to mount and ride,
Booted and spurred, with a heavy stride,
On the opposite shore walked Paul Revere.
Now he patted his horse's side,
Now gazed on the landscape far and near,
Then impetuous stamped the earth,
And turned and tightened his saddle-girth;
But mostly he watched with eager search
The belfry tower of the old North Church,
As it rose above the graves on the hill,
Lonely and spectral and sombre and still.
And lo! as he looks, on the belfry's height,
A glimmer, and then a gleam of light!
He springs to the saddle, the bridle he turns,
But lingers and gazes, till full on his sight
A second lamp in the belfry burns!
A hurry of hoofs in a village street,
A shape in the moonlight, a bulk in the dark,
And beneath from the pebbles, in passing,
      a spark
Struck out by a steed that flies fearless
      and fleet:
That was all! And yet, through the gloom and
      the light,
The fate of a nation was riding that night;
And the spark struck out by that steed, in his
      flight,
Kindled the land into flame with its heat.
He has left the village and mounted the steep,
And beneath him, tranquil and broad and deep,
Is the Mystic, meeting the ocean tides;
And under the alders, that skirt its edge,
Now soft on the sand, now loud on the ledge,
Is heard the tramp of his steed as he rides.

It was twelve by the village clock
When he crossed the bridge into Medford town.
He heard the crowing of the cock,
And the barking of the farmer's dog,

And felt the damp of the river-fog,
That rises when the sun goes down.

It was one by the village clock,
When he galloped into Lexington.
He saw the gilded weathercock
Swim in the moonlight as he passed,
And the meeting-house windows, blank
    and bare,
Gaze at him with a spectral glare,
As if they already stood aghast
At the bloody work they would look upon.

It was two by the village clock,
When he came to the bridge in Concord
    town.
He heard the bleating of the flock,
And the twitter of birds among the trees,
And felt the breath of the morning breeze
Blowing over the meadows brown.
And one was safe and asleep in his bed
Who at the bridge would be first to fall,
Who that day would be lying dead,
Pierced by a British musket-ball.

You know the rest. In the books you have read,
How the British Regulars fired and fled,
How the farmers gave them ball for ball,
From behind each fence and farmyard-wall,
Chasing the red-coats down the lane,
Then crossing the fields to emerge again
Under the trees at the turn of the road,
And only pausing to fire and load.

So through the night rode Paul Revere;
And so through the night went his cry
    of alarm
To every Middlesex village and farm,
A cry of defiance, and not of fear,
A voice in the darkness, a knock at the door,
And a word that shall echo forevermore!
For, borne on the night-wind of the Past,
Through all our history, to the last,
In the hour of darkness and peril and need,
The people will waken and listen to hear
The hurrying hoof-beats of that steed,
And the midnight message of Paul Revere.

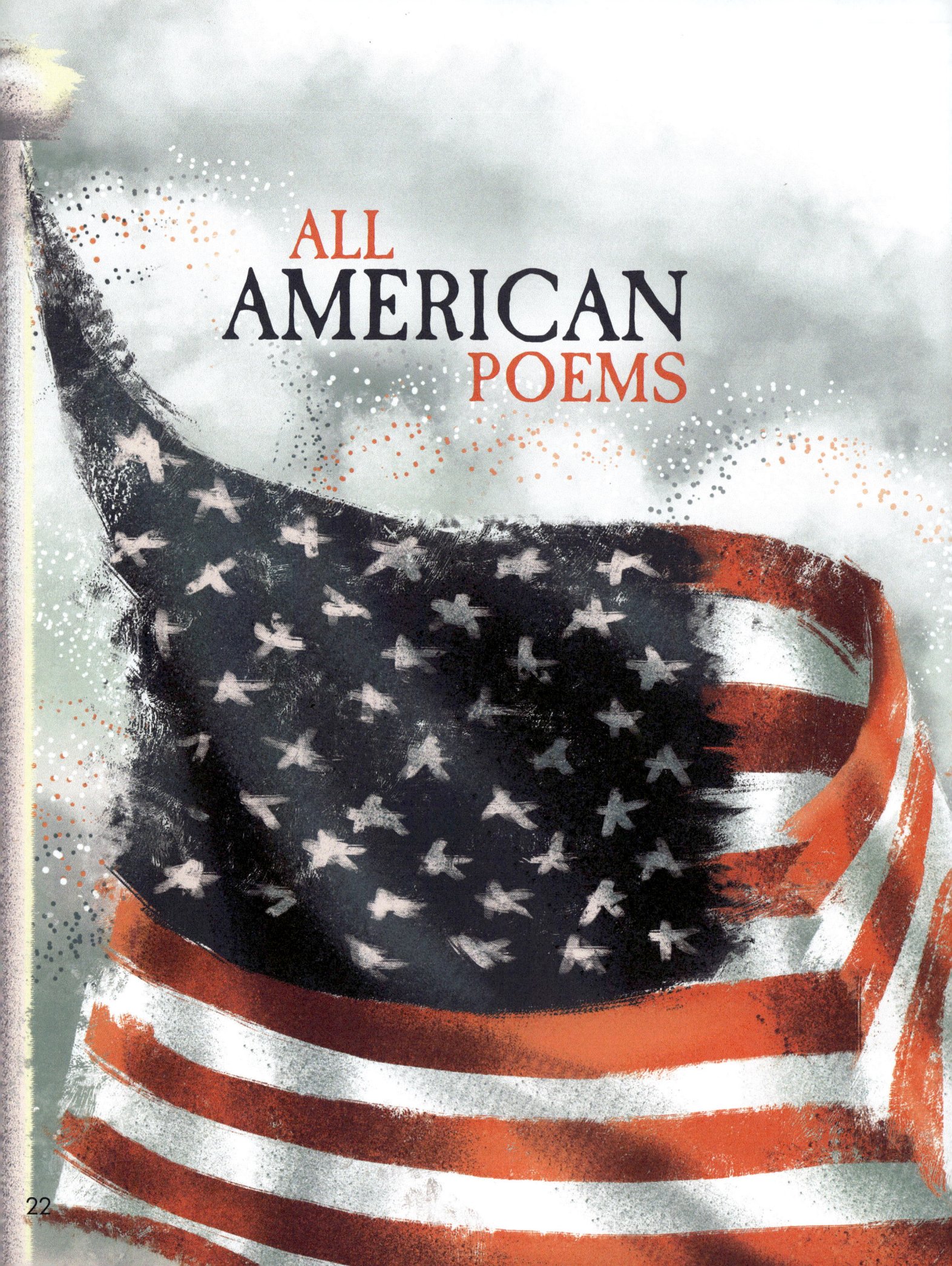

TRACK 16

Two all-American poems celebrating the energy and the drive of life in the United States.

Walt Whitman *served as a battlefield nurse during the American Civil War, and later he wrote movingly and famously about Abraham Lincoln. Whitman wrote poetry to sound like everyday American speech, and he wrote about everyday Americans, setting the scene for later poets such as Robert Frost and Carl Sandburg. Whitman's influence on poets and songwriters is still strong today.*

I Hear America Singing
by Walt Whitman

I hear America singing, the varied carols I hear,
Those of mechanics, each one singing his as it should be blithe and strong,
The carpenter singing his as he measures his plank or beam,
The mason singing his as he makes ready for work, or leaves off work,
The boatman singing what belongs to him in his boat, the deckhand singing on the steamboat deck,
The shoemaker singing as he sits on his bench, the hatter singing as he stands,
The wood-cutter's song, the ploughboy's on his way in the morning, or at noon intermission or at sundown,
The delicious singing of the mother, or of the young wife at work, or of the girl sewing or washing,
Each singing what belongs to him or her and to none else,
The day what belongs to the day—at night the party of young fellows, robust, friendly,
Singing with open mouths their strong melodious songs.

TRACK 17

Ernest Thayer *wrote one famous poem. In 1888, Thayer took that most American of pastimes (a game of baseball) and turned it into a grinning story-poem. Ernest Thayer felt vaguely embarrassed by all the attention. He never published another poem.*

Casey at the Bat
by Ernest Thayer

The outlook wasn't brilliant for the Mudville nine that day:
The score stood four to two, with but one inning more to play,
And then when Cooney died at first, and Barrows did the same,
A pall-like silence fell upon the patrons of the game.

A straggling few got up to go in deep despair. The rest
Clung to the hope which springs eternal in the human breast;
They thought, "If only Casey could but get a whack at that—
We'd put up even money now, with Casey at the bat."

But Flynn preceded Casey, as did also Jimmy Blake,
And the former was a hoodoo, while the latter was a cake;
So upon that stricken multitude grim melancholy sat,
For there seemed but little chance of Casey getting to the bat.

But Flynn let drive a single, to the wonderment of all,
And Blake, the much despisèd, tore the cover off the ball;
And when the dust had lifted, and men saw what had occurred,
There was Jimmy safe at second and Flynn a-hugging third.

Then from five thousand throats and more there rose a lusty yell;
It rumbled through the valley, it rattled in the dell;
It pounded on the mountain and recoiled upon the flat,
For Casey, mighty Casey, was advancing to the bat.

There was ease in Casey's manner as he stepped into his place;
There was pride in Casey's bearing and a smile lit Casey's face.
And when, responding to the cheers, he lightly doffed his hat,
No stranger in the crowd could doubt 'twas Casey at the bat.

Ten thousand eyes were on him as he rubbed his hands with dirt;
Five thousand tongues applauded when he wiped them on his shirt;
Then while the writhing pitcher ground the ball into his hip,
Defiance flashed in Casey's eye, a sneer curled Casey's lip.

And now the leather-covered sphere came hurtling through the air,
And Casey stood a-watching it in haughty grandeur there.
Close by the sturdy batsman the ball unheeded sped—
"That ain't my style," said Casey. "Strike one!" the umpire said.

From the benches, black with people, there went up a muffled roar,
Like the beating of the storm-waves on a stern and distant shore;
"Kill him! Kill the umpire!" shouted someone on the stand;
And it's likely they'd have killed him had not Casey raised his hand.

With a smile of Christian charity great Casey's visage shone;
He stilled the rising tumult; he bade the game go on;
He signaled to the pitcher, and once more the dun sphere flew;
But Casey still ignored it and the umpire said, "Strike two!"

"Fraud!" cried the maddened thousands, and echo answered "Fraud!"
But one scornful look from Casey and the audience was awed.
They saw his face grow stern and cold, they saw his muscles strain,
And they knew that Casey wouldn't let that ball go by again.

The sneer is gone from Casey's lip, his teeth are clenched in hate,
He pounds with cruel violence his bat upon the plate;
And now the pitcher holds the ball, and now he lets it go,
And now the air is shattered by the force of Casey's blow.

Oh, somewhere in this favored land the sun is shining bright,
The band is playing somewhere, and somewhere hearts are light;
And somewhere men are laughing, and somewhere children shout,
But there is no joy in Mudville—mighty Casey has struck out.

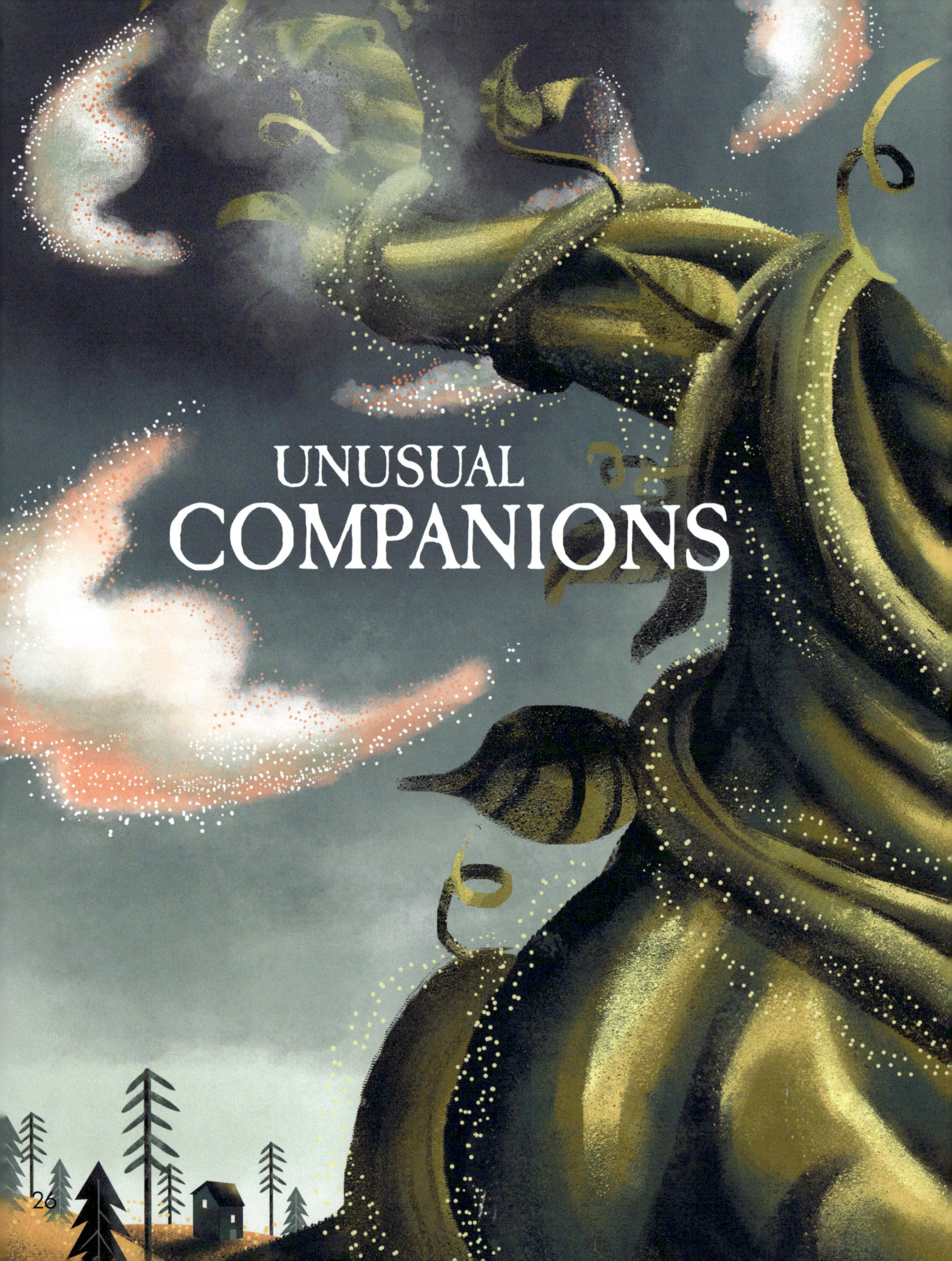

TRACK 18

In this section you're going to hear three poems about a giant, an elf, and... well, I think I'll let you discover the third companion yourself.

The Beanstalk
by Edna St. Vincent Millay

Ho, Giant! This is I!
I have built me a bean-stalk into your
sky!
La—but it's lovely, up so high!

This is how I came—I put
There my knee, here my foot,
Up and up, from shoot to shoot;
And the blessed bean-stalk thinning
Like the mischief all the time,
Till it took me rocking, spinning,
In a dizzy, sunny circle,
Making angles with the root,
Far and out above the cackle
Of the city I was born in;
Till the little dirty city,
In the light so sheer and sunny,
Shone as dazzling bright and pretty
As the money that you find
In a dream of finding money—
What a wind! what a morning!—
Till the tiny, shiny city,
When I shot a glance below
Shaken with a giddy laughter
Sick and blissfully afraid,
Was a dew-drop on a blade,
And a pair of moments after
Was the whirling guess I made;
And the wind was like a whip
Cracking past my icy ears,
And my hair stood out behind,
And my eyes were full of tears,
Wide-open and cold,
More tears than they could hold;
The wind was blowing so,
And my teeth were in a row,
Dry and grinning,
And I felt my foot slip,
And I scratched the wind and whined,
And I clutched the stalk and jabbered
With my eyes shut blind—
What a wind: what a wind!

Your broad sky, Giant,
Is the shelf of a cupboard.
I make bean-stalks—I'm
A builder like yourself;
But bean-stalks is my trade—
I couldn't make a shelf,
Don't know how they're made.
Now, a bean-stalk is more pliant—
La, what a climb!

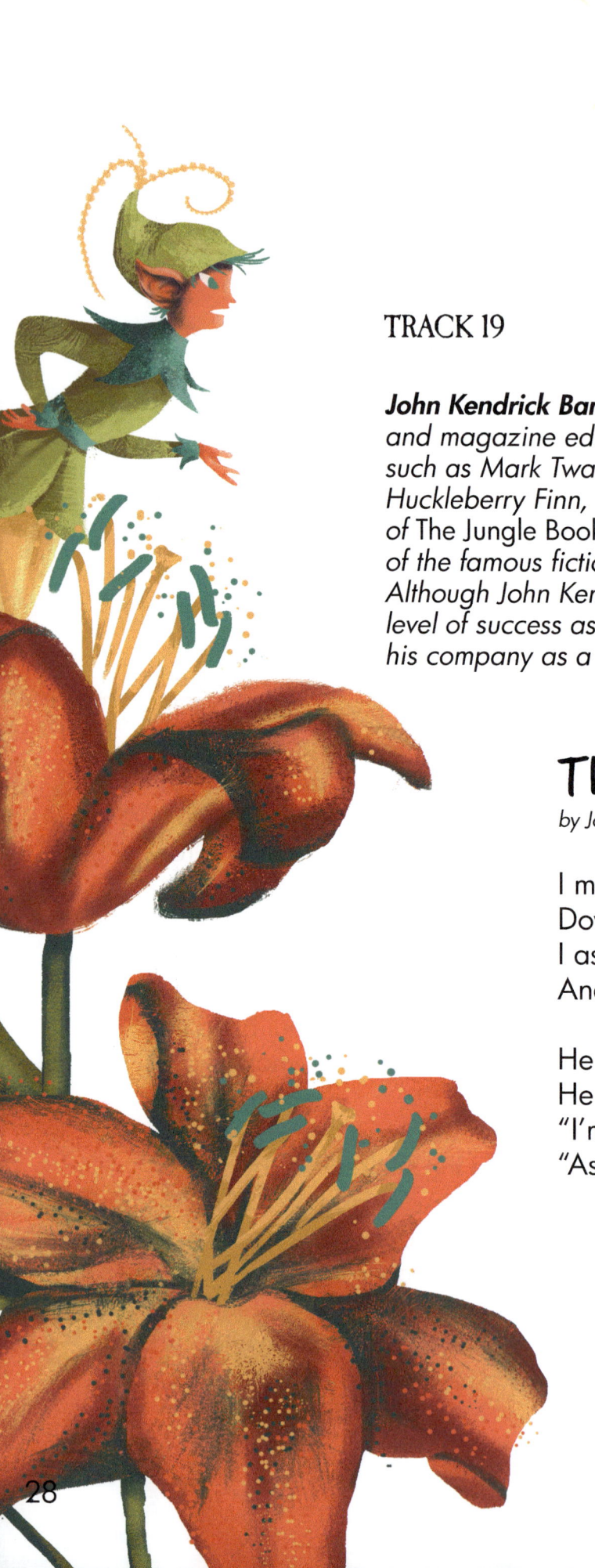

TRACK 19

John Kendrick Bangs was an American writer and magazine editor. His friends included authors such as Mark Twain, creator of Tom Sawyer and Huckleberry Finn, Rudyard Kipling, poet and author of The Jungle Book, and Arthur Conan Doyle, creator of the famous fictional detective Sherlock Holmes. Although John Kendrick Bangs never enjoyed their level of success as a writer, they cordially accepted his company as a friend.

The Little Elf
by John Kendrick Bangs

I met a little Elf-man, once,
Down where the lilies blow.
I asked him why he was so small,
And why he didn't grow.

He slightly frowned, and with his eye
He looked me through and through.
"I'm quite as big for me," said he,
"As you are big for you."

TRACK 20

The Song of the Wandering Aengus
by William Butler Yeats

I went out to the hazel wood,
Because a fire was in my head,
And cut and peeled a hazel wand,
And hooked a berry to a thread;
And when white moths were on the wing,
And moth-like stars were flickering out,
I dropped the berry in a stream
And caught a little silver trout.

When I had laid it on the floor
I went to blow the fire a-flame,
But something rustled on the floor,
And someone called me by my name:
It had become a glimmering girl
With apple blossom in her hair
Who called me by my name and ran
And faded through the brightening air.

Though I am old with wandering
Through hollow lands and hilly lands,
I will find out where she has gone,
And kiss her lips and take her hands;
And walk among long dappled grass,
And pluck till time and times are done,
The silver apples of the moon,
The golden apples of the sun.

POEMS THAT TAKE FLIGHT

TRACK 21

The Eagle
by Alfred, Lord Tennyson

He clasps the crag with crooked hands;
Close to the sun in lonely lands,
Ring'd with the azure world, he stands.
The wrinkled sea beneath him crawls;
He watches from his mountain walls,
And like a thunderbolt he falls.

TRACK 22

The poet who gave us this next piece was **Rachel Field,** *who lived from 1894-1942. Rachel Field was an American poet and novelist and children's novelist, and you may know one of her most famous books, the Newbery Award-winning* Hitty, Her First Hundred Years. *The poem is called...*

Something Told the Wild Geese
by Rachel Field

Something told the wild geese
It was time to go,
Though the fields lay golden
Something whispered, "snow."

Leaves were green and stirring,
Berries, luster-glossed,
But beneath warm feathers
Something cautioned, "frost."

All the sagging orchards
Steamed with amber spice,
But each wild breast stiffened
At remembered ice.

Something told the wild geese
It was time to fly,
Summer sun was on their wings,
Winter in their cry.

TRACK 23

The Swing
by Robert Louis Stevenson

How do you like to go up in a swing,
Up in the air so blue?
Oh, I do think it the pleasantest thing
Ever a child can do!

Up in the air and over the wall,
Till I can see so wide,
River and trees and cattle and all
Over the countryside—

Till I look down on the garden green,
Down on the roof so brown—
Up in the air I go flying again,
Up in the air and down!

INSPIRATION

TRACK 24

Here's an inspiring poem. The poet's name was **Edgar A. Guest,** and he lived from 1881 to 1959. Edgar Guest wrote for a wide, popular public, and that's exactly whom he reached. This poem is simply called:

It Couldn't Be Done
by Edgar A. Guest

Somebody said that it couldn't be done
    But he with a chuckle replied
That "maybe it couldn't," but he would be one
    Who wouldn't say so till he'd tried.
So he buckled right in with the trace of a grin
    On his face. If he worried he hid it.
He started to sing as he tackled the thing
    That couldn't be done, and he did it!

Somebody scoffed: "Oh, you'll never do that;
    At least no one ever has done it;"
But he took off his coat and he took off his hat
    And the first thing we knew he'd begun it.
With a lift of his chin and a bit of a grin,
    Without any doubting or quiddit,
He started to sing as he tackled the thing
    That couldn't be done, and he did it.

There are thousands to tell you it cannot be done,
    There are thousands to prophesy failure,
There are thousands to point out to you one by one,
    The dangers that wait to assail you.
But just buckle in with a bit of a grin,
    Just take off your coat and go to it;
Just start in to sing as you tackle the thing
    That "cannot be done," and you'll do it.

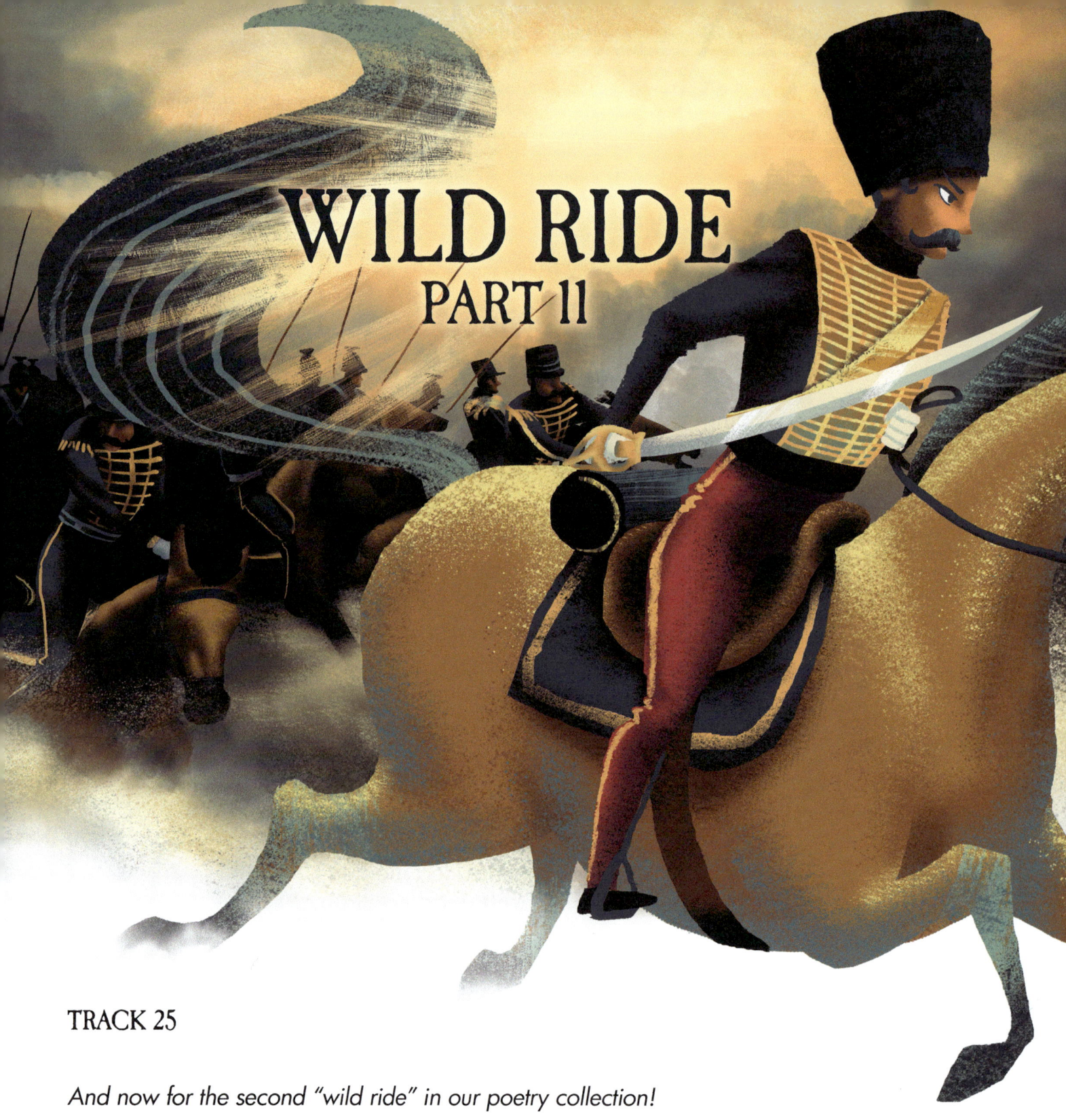

WILD RIDE
PART II

TRACK 25

And now for the second "wild ride" in our poetry collection!

Alfred, Lord Tennyson, was a British aristocrat who wrote in the style of his times, the 1800s. Some of his poems tell stories such as tales of King Arthur and his knights or Greek mythological heroes. "The Charge of the Light Brigade" is one of the greatest of all read-aloud poems, and in it, strangely enough, Tennyson writes thrillingly about one of the stupidest wastes of human life in history, a battle in which a troop of six hundred British cavalry soldiers was ordered to charge against a line of enemy cannons and marksmen, and bravely charged even in the face of nearly certain death.

The Charge of the Light Brigade
by Alfred, Lord Tennyson

Half a league, half a league,
Half a league onward,
All in the valley of Death
   Rode the six hundred.
"Forward, the Light Brigade!
Charge for the guns!" he said.
Into the valley of Death
   Rode the six hundred.

"Forward, the Light Brigade!"
Was there a man dismayed?
Not though the soldier knew
   Someone had blundered.
   Theirs not to make reply,
   Theirs not to reason why,
   Theirs but to do and die.
   Into the valley of Death
   Rode the six hundred.

Cannon to right of them,
Cannon to left of them,
Cannon in front of them
   Volleyed and thundered;
Stormed at with shot and shell,
Boldly they rode and well,
Into the jaws of Death,
Into the mouth of hell
   Rode the six hundred.

Flashed all their sabres bare,
Flashed as they turned in air
Sabring the gunners there,
Charging an army, while
   All the world wondered.
Plunged in the battery-smoke
Right through the line they broke;
Cossack and Russian
Reeled from the sabre stroke
   Shattered and sundered.
Then they rode back, but not
   Not the six hundred.

Cannon to right of them,
Cannon to left of them,
Cannon behind them
   Volleyed and thundered;
Stormed at with shot and shell,
While horse and hero fell.
They that had fought so well
Came through the jaws of Death,
Back from the mouth of hell,
All that was left of them,
   Left of six hundred.

When can their glory fade?
O the wild charge they made!
   All the world wondered.
Honour the charge they made!
Honour the Light Brigade,
   Noble six hundred!

TRACK 26

I call this section of the recording "Sensible Nonsense."

A. A. Milne *was a successful writer of stories and film scripts, poems and plays, but of course he's most famous as the creator of Winnie-the-Pooh, the soft-hearted teddy bear. Milne's books featuring the bear also star a boy, Christopher Robin, who Milne named after his own son, Christopher Robin Milne. Once, when asked how he chose the subjects about which he wrote, Mr. Milne replied, sensibly, "The only excuse which I have yet discovered for writing anything is that I want to write it." Here are two of A. A. Milne's poems.*

Jonathan Jo
by A. A. Milne

Jonathan Jo
Has a mouth like an "O"
And a wheelbarrow full of surprises;
If you ask for a bat
Or for something like that,
He has got it, whatever the size is.

If you're wanting a ball,
It's no trouble at all;
Why, the more that you ask for, the merrier -
Like a hoop and a top,
And a watch that won't stop,
And some sweets, and an Aberdeen terrier.

Jonathan Jo
Has a mouth like an "O,"
But this is what makes him so funny:
If you give him a smile,
Only once in a while,
Then he never expects any money!

The King's Breakfast
by A. A. Milne

The King asked
The Queen, and
The Queen asked
The Dairymaid:
"Could we have some butter for
    The Royal slice of bread?"
The Queen asked the Dairymaid,
The Dairymaid
Said, "Certainly,
I'll go and tell the cow
Now
Before she goes to bed."

The Dairymaid
She curtsied,
And went and told
The Alderney:
"Don't forget the butter for
    The Royal slice of bread."
The Alderney
Said sleepily:
"You'd better tell
His Majesty
That many people nowadays
Like marmalade
Instead."

The Dairymaid
Said, "Fancy!"
And went to
Her Majesty.
She curtsied to the Queen, and
She turned a little red:
"Excuse me,
Your Majesty,
For taking of
The liberty,
But marmalade is tasty, if
It's very
Thickly
Spread."

The Queen said
"Oh!:
And went to
His Majesty:
"Talking of the butter for
    The royal slice of bread,
Many people
Think that
Marmalade
Is nicer.
Would you like to try a little
Marmalade
Instead?"

The King said,
"Bother!"
And then he said,
"Oh, deary me!"
The King sobbed, "Oh, deary me!"
And went back to bed.
"Nobody,"
He whimpered,
"Could call me
A fussy man;
I only want
A little bit

Of butter for
My bread!"

The Queen said,
"There, there!"
And went to
The Dairymaid.
The Dairymaid
Said, "There, there!"
And went to the shed.
The cow said,
"There, there!
I didn't really
Mean it;
Here's milk for his porringer,
And butter for his bread."

The Queen took
The butter
And brought it to
His Majesty;
The King said,
"Butter, eh?"
And bounced out of bed.
"Nobody," he said,
As he kissed her
Tenderly,
"Nobody," he said,
As he slid down the banisters,
"Nobody,
My darling,
Could call me
A fussy man -
BUT
I do like a little bit of butter
    to my bread!"

TRACK 28

Vachel Lindsay was a combination poet and performer. He wrote exciting poems filled with sound effects and surprises, and he became a star performing them in theaters across the USA and Europe. "The Moon's the North Wind's Cooky" is a short example of his work.

The Moon's the North Wind's Cooky (What the Little Girl Said)
by Vachel Lindsay

The Moon's the North Wind's cooky.
He bites it, day by day,
Until there's but a rim of scraps,
That crumble all away.

The South Wind is a baker.
He kneads clouds in his den,
And bakes a crisp new moon that...greedy
North...Wind...eats...again!

*The English poet **Edward Lear** had a marvelous sense of humor. He made up amusing new words and used old words in amusing new ways. Here is one of my favorite Edward Lear poems, but you really ought to look for more.*

The Pobble Who Has No Toes
by Edward Lear

The Pobble who has no toes
    Had once as many as we;
When they said, "Some day you may
    lose them all;"
    He replied, "Fish fiddle de-dee!"
And his Aunt Jobiska made him drink,
Lavender water tinged with pink,
For she said, "The World in general knows
There's nothing so good for a Pobble's toes!"

The Pobble who has no toes,
    Swam across the Bristol Channel;
But before he set out he wrapped his nose,
    In a piece of scarlet flannel.
For his Aunt Jobiska said, "No harm
Can come to his toes if his nose is warm;
And it's perfectly known that a Pobble's toes
Are safe, — provided he minds his nose."

The Pobble swam fast and well
    And when boats or ships came near him
He tinkedly-binkledy-winkled a bell
    So that all the world could hear him.
And all the Sailors and Admirals cried,
When they saw him nearing the further side, —
"He has gone to fish, for his Aunt Jobiska's
Runcible Cat with crimson whiskers!"

But before he touched the shore,
    The shore of the Bristol Channel,
A sea-green Porpoise carried away
    His wrapper of scarlet flannel.
And when he came to observe his feet
Formerly garnished with toes so neat
His face at once became forlorn
On perceiving that all his toes were gone!

And nobody ever knew
    From that dark day to the present,
Whoso had taken the Pobble's toes,
    In a manner so far from pleasant.
Whether the shrimps or crawfish gray,
Or crafty Mermaids stole them away —
Nobody knew; and nobody knows
How the Pebble was robbed of his
    twice five toes!

The Pobble who has no toes
    Was placed in a friendly Bark,
And they rowed him back, and carried him up,
    To his Aunt Jobiska's Park.
And she made him a feast at his earnest wish
Of eggs and buttercups fried with fish; —
And she said, — "It's a fact the whole
    world knows,
That Pobbles are happier without their toes."

TRACK 30

*Earlier, we shared a poem by **Robert Louis Stevenson** called "Windy Nights," followed by another poem on the same subject called "Who Has Seen the Wind?" Now let's share a second pair of poems.*

Once again we'll hear from Robert Louis Stevenson, whom you may remember spent much of his childhood ill and in bed. His poem here is called "Bed In Summer." You'll also hear Thomas Hood's poem "In the Summer When I Go To Bed."

Bed In Summer
by Robert Louis Stevenson

In winter I get up at night
And dress by yellow candle-light.
In summer, quite the other way,
I have to go to bed by day.

I have to go to bed and see
The birds still hopping on the tree,
Or hear the grown-up people's feet
Still going past me in the street.

And does it not seem hard to you,
When all the sky is clear and blue,
And I should like so much to play,
To have to go to bed by day?

Thomas Hood was a British poet of the late 1800s who wrote two totally different kinds of poetry. He wrote dramatic poems about poor hard-working people struggling through tough times, and those poems helped create public support for laws and programs to help real people in need. Thomas Hood's other poems were gentle humorous pieces such as "In the Summer When I Go To Bed."

In the Summer When I Go To Bed
by Thomas Hood

In the summer when I go to bed
The sun still streaming overhead
My bed becomes so small and hot
With sheets and pillow in a knot
And then I lie and try to see
The things I'd really like to be.

I think I'd be a glossy cat
A little plump, but not too fat,
I'd never touch a bird or mouse
I'm much too busy 'round the house.

And then a fierce and hungry hound
The king of dogs for miles around
I'd chase the postman just for fun
To see how quickly he could run.

Perhaps I'd be a crocodile
Within the marshes of the Nile
And paddle in the river-bed
With dripping mud-caps on my head.

Or maybe next a mountain goat,
With shaggy whiskers at my throat,
Leaping streams and jumping rocks
In stripey pink and purple socks.

Or else I'd be a polar bear
And on an iceberg make my lair;
I'd keep a shop in Baffin Sound
To sell icebergs by the pound.

And then I'd be a wise old frog,
Squatting on a sunken log,
I'd teach the fishes lots of games
And how to read and write their names.

An Indian lion then I'd be
And lounge about on my settee;
I'd feed on nothing but bananas
And spend all day in my pyjamas.

I'd like to be a tall giraffe
Making lots of people laugh;
I'd do a tap-dance in the street
With little bells upon my feet.

And then I'd be a foxy fox
Streaking through the hollyhocks;
Horse or hound would ne'er catch me
I'm a master of disguise, you see.

I think I'd be a chimpanzee
With musical ability,
I'd play a silver clarinet
Or form a Monkey String Quartet.

And then a snake with scales of gold
Guarding hoards of wealth untold,
No thief would dare to steal a pin —
But friends of mine I would let in.

But then before I really know
Just what I'd be or where I'd go
My bed becomes so wide and deep
And all my thoughts are fast asleep.

TRACK 32

The much-loved poet **Eugene Field** was born in St. Louis, Missouri, the son of an equally famous father. Roswell Martin Field was a successful lawyer. In the 1850s, he represented in court the African-American slave Dred Scott, who brought a lawsuit demanding his own freedom. The loss of that case drove so many citizens to take an active role in trying to end slavery in the USA that the Dred Scott case became known as "The Lawsuit that Started the Civil War."

Despite his father's involvement in such serious events, Eugene Field grew up a light-hearted soul. For a time he became a newspaper journalist, but his sense of humor was too strong to be ignored. Soon he began publishing humorous poems for family enjoyment, and it was his dozen volumes of poetry that made Eugene Field famous and wealthy. Today his boyhood home in St. Louis is a museum, and scattered across the USA are dozens of schools named after this master of children's literature.

"Wynken, Blynken, and Nod" is one of Eugene Field's most beloved poems.

Wynken, Blynken, and Nod
by Eugene Field

Wynken, Blynken, and Nod one night
   Sailed off in a wooden shoe,—
Sailed on a river of crystal light
   Into a sea of dew.
"Where are you going, and what do you
     wish?"
   The old moon asked the three.
"We have come to fish for the herring-fish
   That live in this beautiful sea;
Nets of silver and gold have we,"
      Said Wynken,
      Blynken,
      And Nod.

The old moon laughed and sang a song,
   As they rocked in the wooden shoe;
And the wind that sped them all night long
   Ruffled the waves of dew;
The little stars were the herring-fish
   That lived in the beautiful sea.
"Now cast your nets wherever you wish,—
   Never afraid are we!"
So cried the stars to the fishermen three,
      Wynken,
      Blynken,
      And Nod.

All night long their nets they threw
   To the stars in the twinkling foam,—
Then down from the skies came the wooden
     shoe,
   Bringing the fishermen home:
'Twas all so pretty a sail, it seemed
   As if it could not be;
And some folk thought 'twas a dream they'd
     dreamed
   Of sailing that beautiful sea;
But I shall name you the fishermen three:
      Wynken,
      Blynken,
      And Nod.

Wynken and Blynken are two little eyes,
   And Nod is a little head,
And the wooden shoe that sailed the skies
   Is a wee one's trundle-bed;
So shut your eyes while Mother sings
   Of wonderful sights that be,
And you shall see the beautiful things
   As you rock in the misty sea
   Where the old shoe rocked the fishermen
     three:—
      Wynken,
      Blynken,
      And Nod.

TRACK 33

Leigh Hunt, who lived from 1784 to 1859, counted as friends almost all of the greatest British writers of his time. "Abou Ben Adhem" tells a made-up version of the true story of a king who lived about two thousand years ago in what today we call Afghanistan, and who became famous for helping others.

Abou Ben Adhem
by Leigh Hunt

Abou Ben Adhem (may his tribe increase!)
Awoke one night from a deep dream of peace,
And saw, within the moonlight in his room,
Making it rich, and like a lily in bloom,
An angel writing in a book of gold:
Exceeding peace had made Ben Adhem bold,
And to the presence in the room he said,
"What writest thou?" — The vision raised its head,
And with a look made of all sweet accord,
Answered, "The names of those who love the Lord."
"And is mine one?" said Abou. "Nay, not so,"
Replied the angel. Abou spoke more low,
But cheerily still; and said, "I pray thee, then,
Write me as one that loves his fellow men."

The angel wrote, and vanished. The next night
It came again with a great wakening light,
And showed the names whom love of God had blest,
And lo! Ben Adhem's name led all the rest.

TRACK 34

CONCLUSION

I hope you've enjoyed this presentation from Well Trained Mind Press of *Heroes, Horses, and Harvest Moons: A Cornucopia of Best-Loved Poems, Volume One*. For more award-winning recordings and books from Jim Weiss and from Well-Trained Mind, please go to our website, welltrainedmind.com, or call toll-free 877-322-3445.

Thank you for listening.